This Little Tiger book belongs to:

_____

_____

_____

For my good friend Elaine
~ C. F.

For Grandma, with love.
~ J. M.

LITTLE TIGER PRESS
1 The Coda Centre, 189 Munster Road, London SW6 6AW
www.littletigerpress.com

First published in Great Britain 2003
by Little Tiger Press, London
This edition published 2012

Printed in China

2 4 6 8 10 9 7 5 3 1

Night-Night, Poppy!

Claire Freedman

Jane Massey

LITTLE TIGER PRESS

It was bedtime, but Poppy couldn't find her favorite bear, Growly Ted. She'd looked everywhere.

Mommy had to tuck her in
with Quacky Duck instead.
"Night-night, Poppy, night-night,
Quacky Duck," said Mommy.
"Night-night, Mommy and
Quacky Duck," said Poppy.
"Quack-quack!" quacked Quacky Duck.

Poppy would have fallen fast
asleep right then. But OH, NO!
The bed didn't feel quite right.
So Poppy went to find Furry Cat.

"Night-night, Quacky Duck
and Furry Cat," said Poppy.
"Meow," purred Furry Cat.
"Quack-quack," quacked
Quacky Duck.

Poppy would have fallen fast asleep that
very minute. But OH, NO! The bed STILL
didn't feel quite right. It felt too empty.
  Out Poppy climbed to look for Hooty Owl.

"Night-night," Poppy told Hooty Owl, Furry Cat, and Quacky Duck.

"Whoo, whoo," hooted Hooty Owl.

"Meow," purred Furry Cat.

"Quack-quack," quacked Quacky Duck. "Quack!"

Poppy would have fallen asleep in a flash.
But OH, NO! Now the bed felt too cold.
   Where was Dimple Dog?
   Poppy found him downstairs, behind
the curtains.

"Night-night, Dimple Dog and
Hooty Owl," said Poppy. "Night-night,
Furry Cat and Quacky Duck."
   "Woof-woof," barked Dimple Dog.
   "Whoo, whoo," hooted Hooty Owl.
   "Meow," purred Furry Cat.
     Quacky Duck didn't say a word.
He was already fast asleep.

Poppy would have fallen fast asleep, too.
But OH, NO! Now the bed covers felt too loose.
Poppy crept out to find Woolly Lamb.

"Night-night, everyone," said Poppy.
"Baa-baa," bleated Woolly Lamb.
"Woof-woof," barked Dimple Dog.
"Whoo, whoo," hooted Hooty Owl.
"Meow," purred Furry Cat.
"Quack-quack," quacked Quacky Duck,
who'd woken up again with all the noise.

Now Poppy would have fallen fast
asleep in an instant. But OH, NO!
She just couldn't get comfy.
The pillow felt all lumpy.
  "What's under here?" said Poppy.
"Oh, so that's where you've been
hiding, silly Growly Ted!"

Then Poppy put
Quacky Duck
back in the toy box.

She propped
Furry Cat back
up on his shelf.

She put Hooty Owl
back under
the bed.

And she carried
Dimple Dog
and Woolly Lamb
back downstairs.

Then Poppy and Growly Ted settled
down together under the covers.
  "Night-night, Growly Ted," yawned
Poppy.
  "Grrr!" growled Growly Ted.
And Poppy fell fast asleep. OH, YES!
Because the bed felt just right.

And Growly Ted
would have fallen fast asleep
that same second too.
But OH, NO! . . .

Suddenly the bed
was far too full!
"Grrrr!"